Vote for Duck

Doreen Cronin
Illustrated by Betsy Lewin

Simon & Schuster

London   New York   Sydney

**SIMON &
SCHUSTER**

First published in Great Britain in 2004 by Simon & Schuster UK Ltd ★ Africa House, 64-78 Kingsway, London WC2B 6AH
★ Originally published in 2004 by Simon & Schuster Books for Young Readers, an imprint of Simon & Schuster Children's
Publishing Division, New York ★ Text copyright © 2004 Doreen Cronin ★ Illustrations copyright © 2004 Betsy Lewin ★ The
right of Doreen Cronin and Betsy Lewin to be identified as the author and illustrator of this work has been asserted by them
in accordance with the Copyright, Designs and Patents Act, 1988★ Book design by Dan Potash ★ The text for this book is set
in Filosofia ★ The illustrations for this book are rendered in brush and watercolour ★ All rights reserved, including the right
of reproduction in whole or in part in any form ★ A CIP catalogue record for this book is available from the British Library
upon request ★ ISBN 0-689-86041-2 ★ Manufactured in the United States of America ★ 10 9 8 7 6 5 4 3 2 1

For Cathy — *D. C.*　　　　To life, liberty, and the pursuit of happiness — *B. L.*

Running a farm is very hard work.

At the end of each day Farmer Brown is covered from head to toe in hay, seeds, grass, feathers, filth, mud, muck and coffee stains.

He doesn't smell very good, either.

The animals have chores to do, too.

PIGS– CLEAN UNDER THE BEDS

COWS– WEED THE GARDEN

SHEEP– SWEEP THE BARN

DUCK– MOW THE LAWN
TAKE OUT THE RUBBISH
GRIND THE COFFEE BEANS

At the end of each day,
the pigs are covered in fluff.
The cows are covered in weeds.
The sheep are covered in dust.

**And Duck is covered in tiny bits of grass
and espresso beans.**

Duck did not like to do chores.
He did not like picking tiny bits of grass and espresso
beans out of his feathers.
"Why is Farmer Brown in charge, anyway?" thought Duck.
"What we need is an election!"
He made a sign and hung it up in the barn.

The next morning, Farmer Brown found a poster on his front door.

Farmer Brown was furious.
He ran to the barn and found the animals
registering to vote.

The mice got together and protested against the height requirement. So Duck crossed it off.

On Election Day, each of the animals marked
a ballot paper and placed it in a box.
The vote was counted and the results were
posted on the barn wall.

Farmer Brown demanded a recount.

One sticky ballot was found
stuck to the bottom of a pig.

The new tally was:

F. Brown 6
DUCK 21

The voters had spoken.

Duck was officially in charge.

Running a farm is very hard work.

At the end of each day, Duck was covered from head to toe in hay, seeds, grass, feathers, filth, mud, muck and coffee stains.

"Running a farm is no fun at all," thought Duck.

That night Duck and his staff started working
on Duck's campaign for governor.

Duck left Farmer Brown in charge and
hit the campaign trail.

He visited small-town diners.

He marched in parades.

He went to town meetings.

He gave speeches that only other ducks could understand.

On Election Day, the voters marked their ballot papers in polling booths all over the state.

The vote was counted and the results were posted in the local paper.

The governor demanded a recount.

Two sticky ballots were found stuck to
the bottom of a plate of pancakes.

The new tally was:

MS. Governor
299,999

DUCK 300,002

The voters had spoken.

Duck was officially in charge.

Running a state is very hard work.

At the end of each day, Duck was covered
from head to toe in hairspray, inkstains,
fingerprints, mayonnaise and coffee stains.

And he had a very bad headache.

"Running a state is no fun at all," thought Duck.

That night Duck and his staff started working on posters for the presidential election.

Duck left his staff in charge and hit the campaign trail.

**He kissed babies
in local diners.**

He marched in parades.

He gave speeches that only
other ducks could understand.

He even played the saxophone on late-night television.

On Election Day, the voters marked their ballot papers in polling booths all over the country.

The vote was counted and the results were announced on the news.

Decision America

MR. PRESIDENT
50,546,165
DUCK
50,546,170

. . . DUCK DEFEATS PRESIDENT . . .

The president demanded a recount.
Ten sticky ballots were found stuck to
the bottom of the vice president.

The new tally was:

Decision America

MR. PRESIDENT
50,546,165
DUCK
50,546,180

. . DUCK STILL DEFEATS PRESIDENT .

The voters had spoken. Duck was officially in charge.

Running a country
is very hard work.

At the end of each day
Duck was covered from
head to toe in face powder,
paper cuts, staples,
security badges,
secret-service agents
and coffee stains.

And he had a very bad
headache.

"Running a country is no
fun at all," thought Duck.

Then he checked the small ads in the paper:

★ **DUCK NEEDED** ★
No experience necessary.
Must be able to mow the lawn
and grind coffee beans.

Duck left the vice president in charge
and headed back to the farm.

At the end of each day Farmer Brown is now covered
from head to toe in hay, seeds, grass, feathers, filth,
mud, muck and coffee stains.

And Duck . . .

. . . is working on his autobiography.